Christmas in Catland

Alice Goyder

CHATTO & WINDUS · LONDON

Tilly and Minnie were stirring the Christmas pudding. Each made a wish.
What did they wish? Wishes are secret and if you tell they don't come true.

Tilly and Minnie wrapped up their presents.
The presents were secrets too.
But they squeezed them and shook them
and prodded them and tried to guess
what they were.

Mother Grimalkin took Minnie to see Mr. Poulter. They bought a plump turkey that was almost as big as Minnie.

That afternoon Tilly and Minnie helped their Mother Grimalkin to hang a big sprig of mistletoe from the ceiling.
'Now everyone can kiss under the mistletoe,' said Mother Grimalkin.

Next morning, Grandfather Grimalkin arrived. He wore a black top hat. Grandmother Grimalkin was well wrapped up in her fur coat and Aunt Millicent wore a blue bonnet with a bow.

Christmas Eve!
Tilly and Minnie had hung up their stockings.
They both tried to stay awake for as long
as possible, but when Father Christmas
arrived with his reindeer, they were both
sound asleep!

Ding-dong-ding-dong!
The church bells rang out on Christmas
morning. And there were the stockings
all swollen and bursting with good things.

After breakfast, they all went skating on the frozen pond. How very cold and how very hard the ice was! They wobbled and slithered and panted and laughed all morning.

What a Christmas feast!
There was turkey and ham and mince pies
and plum pudding and nuts and grapes.
'It is time to open the presents,'
Father Grimalkin cried.

Under the Christmas tree were two
beautiful rocking horses!
'Just what I wished for!' cried Tilly.
'Just what I wished for!' shouted Minnie.
They had both had the same wish.

That night they dreamed they were riding the rocking horses way up in the sky to a land beyond the clouds where it was always Christmas.

Published by
Chatto and Windus Ltd
40 William IV Street, London WC2N 4DF

✳

Clarke, Irwin & Co Ltd, Toronto

Edited, designed and produced by
Culford Books
135 Culford Road, London N1

©Rosemary Goldsmith 1978

First published 1978

ISBN 0 7011 2347 8

Printed and bound by
Waterlow (Dunstable) Ltd, England